IN A CERTAIN KINGDOM

Epic Heroes of the Rus

NICHOLAS KOTAR

WAYSTONE
PRESS

The Childhood of Ilya Muromets

🙠🙢

I n a certain kingdom, in a certain land, there lived a farmer, named Ivan Timofeevich, and his wife Evfrosinia Alexandrovna. For many years, they lamented that they had no child of their own. It was a source of hidden grief for both, for Ivan had no son to push the plow when he got old, and Evfrosinia could look to no support in her old age.

But one night, a new star shone in the night sky, brighter than the sun, more luminous than the moon. The prayers of the parents were answered. A little boy was born to them; Ilya they named him.

Immediately, Ivan Timofeevich called together all his neighbors, all his friends, even those who lived in the village over the hill and past the river. He called them all to share his joy. And just to make sure they all came, he asked the great warrior-farmer himself, Mikula Selianinovich, to be godfather.

And so, one bright summer day, the village feasted. A pile of silver spoons lay on a trestle table outside, and every guest gave what baptism-price he could. Some gave a penny, some a handful. But Mikula Selianinovich gave a whole golden coin.

And they sat to eat, food in varieties most of them had never seen before. Evfrosinia Alexandrovna, dressed in her finest, came with a silver goblet of the finest wine and passed it to her husband Ivan. And he, in turn, passed it to the godfather. Mikula, a mighty man, left the dregs at the bottom. Then he hurled them up at the branches of the trees and intoned,

> *"Don't come back to earth, you drops of fine wine.*
> *Grow into ripened fruits on the branches,*
> *So that Ilyusha himself,*
> *Tall and strong as a warrior*
> *Can pluck them down with his own hands*
> *As he sits astride his great warrior horse."*

At those words, Ilya woke up in his crib and screamed. The shutters flew back, the house rocked on its foundations, a wind pushed back the hair of the feasters.

And they laughed.

"Too early, Ilyusha," they said. "You can't have your horse yet. First you must learn to walk!"

How little did they know, those carefree feasters, that their words would be a prophecy of woe.

Three years passed. The grass grew green in patches over the brown, the rivers overflowed their banks, but only slightly. The birches burst into their feathery tears of early spring. And Ilyusha rode the shoulders of his godfather Mikula as he showed him the wonders of his glorious Rus. There he pointed at the gables and crosses of Kiev, there, the towers and domes of Novgorod the beautiful. There the endless banks of the Volga—more sea than river, there the wide and smooth water of the Dniepr.

But Ilyusha only wanted to run, to feel the dew on his bare feet. And his godfather let him. No one could naysay the little warrior, so strong was his spirit, even in that little body of his.

As the sun started its way down, Ilya finally grew tired. Mikula picked him up by the side of the road, but to do so, he put down the pack he had on his back. And he forgot it on the side of the road, so filled with joy was he at his little warrior-godson.

As they walked back home, the trees behind them creaked and shook. The mountains groaned. The wind wailed. A giant warrior rode through the forest on his giant horse. The tip of his helm grazed the clouds, and every time his horse shook its mane, lightning flashed and thunder boomed.

This was the giant Kalivan, a name that struck fear in everyone—friend and foe alike.

"Oh my burden," he cried, lamenting. "Oh the heaviness of my sorrow. For what can I do with this, my terrible strength? If only there were a ring stuck into the bones of Mother Earth. I would pull on that ring, and turn the earth itself inside out."

The giant warrior and his giant horse turned to the road. Kalivan saw the pack that Mikula had left behind. He nudged it with his sword, but the pack wouldn't budge. Curious, the giant dismounted. The earth shook and dust came up in whirling clouds as he did, but the pack wouldn't budge. He nudged it with his toe. He shook it with his fist. He pulled it with both hands. Nothing. The pack simply wouldn't move.

Delighted at the challenge, Kalivan rolled up his sleeves and pulled. At last! The pack lifted a fraction, but he couldn't manage to hold it up. It crashed back down. And he found he was buried down to his shins in Mother Earth herself.

Perplexed, annoyed, but still up for the challenge, Kalivan pulled again. It lifted up a handbreadth! But now he was buried in earth to his thighs.

At that moment, Mikula, with Ilya still on his shoulders, came back into view, intent on getting back the pack he forgot on the side of the road. He stopped in shock at the sight of Kalivan the great, half-buried in the dirt.

"What a sight is this!" he said, and as he did, he picked up the pack and hoisted it on his shoulder as though it weighed no more than a feather.

"How did you do that?" bellowed Kalivan. "I am the strongest man in the world. And yet, I could not budge it!"

"Tell me, great one! For what do you use your great strength that God Himself gave you? Do you use it for truth, for virtue, for righteousness?"

"What truth?" scoffed Kalivan. "What virtue do you speak of? All the righteousness I know is this: that I have power like no one else, that others must quail before it. That all below me are slaves to my will, for no one is man enough to stand up to me! That is my truth, you foolish peasant!"

Turning to Ilyusha at his shoulder, Mikula said, "Listen, Ilyusha. There is nothing in this pack, nothing save the earth herself. The honest dirt of honest labors of honest hands. And it is stronger than all the might of all the warriors of this earth put together."

At those words, Kalivan groaned from pain. But that cry was cut short, for Kalivan the great had turned into a mountain.

Ilya kept these words in his heart, or as much as his childish heart could take.

But soon he would have more time than most to think. For a sickness struck the child-warrior. The apple of his parents' eyes lost the use of all his limbs. Wide-eyed and sallow-faced, he sat at the window and watched. And watched. He could do nothing else.

The rivers flowed on, through spring after spring. Every winter, it seemed that the ice would never break, but every year, one miraculous day, some ineffable spark in the air cracked the wall, and the water flowed again.

But none of this would Ilya every see. For he sat, his limbs useless, at the window, as his parents aged early, weighed down by work and toil and the inexorable taskmaster of grief. And their land, once a glistening Eden, became a vale of thorns and tears.

But spring still came. The waters still flowed. And one

morning, after Ivan left before the sun to his thankless toil, and Evfrosinia was out in the fields with her husband, Ilya was awoken from fitful sleep.

"Up! Get up, Ilya Muromets! Up! Get up! Open the door to us, wandering folk!"

Was it real, or was it a dream?

"Up! Get up, Ilya Muromets! What shame to lie in laziness when those older and frailer than you wait at the gates! Open them!"

And Ilya got up! And he stood on his own two feet! And they held his weight, and they even held him as he shifted into a lurching walk.

The gate gave way before his fingers as though it were paper. The sun shone on his head for the first time in years. It dazzled him as he stared at the hobbled forms of three old men in travelers' garb. Each of them held a wooden drinking vessel carved in the shape of a mallard.

"Welcome," said the first of the old men. "Welcome, Ilya, to the world of the living. Come, drink of this mead that the bees themselves toiled over in their sun-drenched fields."

Ilya drank deeply from the first vessel.

His heart filled with joy, his arms filled with strength, his soul filled with rejoicing

The second old traveler gave Ilya to drink. Ilya drank deeply from the second vessel.

"What do you feel, Ilya Muromets?"

"Oh wonder! My arms and my legs—they fill with life as though they were a wineskin."

The third old traveler gave Ilya to drink. Ilya drank deeply from the third vessel.

"What do you feel, Ilya Muromets?"

"Oh wonder! All my aches and pains are gone as though they never were."

"Come back to life, young warrior. May you never again feel sickness and pain. Now go, Ilya Muromets. Go to the swift river, Karacharovo. Bring us a vessel of cold spring water."

And the young warrior did, bringing back a full bucket.

The old travelers drank their fill, and they gave him to drink as well.

"And what about now, young Ilya?"

"Oh, wonder! I feel the strength of ten men in my bones, the power of ten in my muscles."

"Bring us some more of that cold spring water."

The young warrior did, bringing back a full bucket.

The old travelers drank their fill, and they gave him to drink as well.

"And what about now, young Ilya?"

"My word! What strength now fills me! The power of hundreds in my blood and body. If I saw a stump in front of me, and in that stump was a ring of iron, I would pick the earth herself up and swing her about my head."

The three old travelers looked at each other in consternation. "Oh dear. We've done a bit too much, haven't we? No, Ilyusha, no man should have strength like that. Go and bring us some more of that cold spring water."

The young warrior did, bringing back a full bucket.

The old wanderers drank their fill, then carefully they gave the rest to Ilya.

"And how do you feel now, my young warrior?"

"I feel half of my previous strength," he said.

"It is enough," they said and sighed heavily. "Now hear our words, Ilya Muromets, and listen well to our counsel. This is a God-given gift you have, to do with as you will. You can use it to plow the earth or for some other worthy craft. If you wish, you may go to battle. For it is said that you will not die from the sword of a fellow-warrior.

"But hear our warning as well. Go and fight all who dare to raise arms against our Mother Rus. But never start a fight with Sviatogor the great, for Mother Earth herself groans under the weight of his walking. Don't pick a quarrel with Krasnoiar, for his lot it is to smith the fates of men. And never raise a hand against Mikula Selianinovich, for Mother Earth loves him as her own. And whatever you do, steer clear of Volga Vseslav'evich. For if he cannot best you in strength, he will outwit you. And if he cannot outwit you, he will beat you with cunning."

And so saying, the old wanderers disappeared. Were they even there in the first place?

The strength flowed through young Ilya like his own lifeblood. And the joy burst from him like the sun breaking through winter clouds.

He turned to his father's land. It was filled with stumps and old fallen trees and broken branches and fissures in the badly-turned earth. For Ivan Timofeevich was only a man, not a bogatyr like his son. And Ilya went to work with a fury like winter itself in the middle of March.

The land was done, the fissures filled, the old trees uprooted and chopped into piles enough to last them for years on end! And still Ilyusha was not tired. So he did the same to all his neighbors, all those who long ago had paid for the spoons at his baptism.

And he finished, and still he was filled to the brim with power and strength, the joy spilling out of him like mead from a bucket.

And he turned to his own dear home. It was in a sorry state. The roof had fallen in in places. The foundations were cracked. The window panes were splintered and dirty.

And he went to work with a fury like a storm in early April.

Then Ivan Timofeevich came home, Evfrosinia Alexandrovna with him. What a wonder met their eyes! A roof newly-shingled. A bucking horse on the crossbeam. A new banya with a mountain of wood for the stove.

Then Ilyusha asked the blessing of his parents. They wept over him, fussed over him like hens over a golden egg. But they let him go. For his fate was yet to be made.

And he went to his godfather Mikula Selianinovich for counsel.

"Ilyusha, Ilyusha," he said. "Little could I have guessed that my toast at your baptism would come out so well! Now hie from this place, go to my brother Krasnoiar for a new set of mail. Go to Sviatogor for a sword and a blessing. And then go out to the roads, for is it not your calling to guard our great mother, Rus the bright? Who else will protect the borders and fight off the heathen? But first, a horse!"

And Mikula laughed as he remembered Ilyusha's baby-cry at the baptism, when he had mentioned his future warrior-horse.

"Go to the road, Ilyusha, past Murom-city. The first trader you meet, buy a foal from him. Feed him, care for him for three months. Take him out at night, so the dew of the mountains can soak his black coat. Then take him to a fencepost and sit on him. If he can clear the fencepost, you have your warrior-horse, my boy!"

And so he did. The foal grew not by days, but by hours, and Ilyusha had a great black warhorse. And he loved him as though the foal were his own dear brother.

Finally he came to his mother and father. Sensing the ending of his time at home, Evfrosinia wept. But Ivan blessed his son and charged him never to abuse his strength, to remember the age-old lesson of Kalivan's pride.

And on rode Ilya, following the sun as it set, on his way to Krasnoiar for a new set of mail. But what he was to find there at the feet of great Sviatogor, he would never have guessed. But that is a tale for another time.

How Ilya Muromets Received Sviatogor's Sword

❦

I lya Muromets sat on his new warrior horse and rode north, all the way to the distant mountains that grazed the tips of the sky.

Under those mountains stood an old oak, intertwining with itself in a maze of branches. Under that oak stood a forge, and in that forge the bellows blew loudly, the fire came up from the chimney in bursts. Next to that fire stood a great warrior—Krasnoiar, brother to Mikula Selianinovich—beating the metal with a hammer larger than any hammer Ilya had ever seen.

Krasnoiar greeted Ilya and wasted no time. Immediately, he took to forging a new mail shirt for Rus's newest protector of the ways. A helm he beat out of metal, greaves shining and hot, a mail shirt and a spear. He even forged a metal quiver for a flock of metal arrows.

Only one thing he could not make, no matter how hard he tried. He forged a sword, but it cracked in the heat. He forged another, but it shattered in water. Nothing could he do. Not a single piece of metal gave itself to become Ilya's new sword.

Perplexed, Krasnoiar turned to Ilyusha.

"It seems, young man, that you have only one path to

follow. Go to the great Sviatogor, the mountainous warrior. It is time for him to relinquish his sword, for you to take his place. And don't worry, that sword is my best work."

And so, Ilya traveled on, deeper into the mountains. In those mountains, those holy mountains, lived a wondrous bogatyr, a warrior that even Mother Earth could no longer bear. Sviatogor no longer rode on the plains of Mother Rus, but could only walk on the peaks, lest the earth itself shatter under his mountainous feet.

Ilya Muromets rode on, and from a distance he saw the giant warrior, great as a mountain. His helm grazed the tips of the clouds. He rode a mountainous horse, and every time that horse shook its mane, thunder boomed and lightning flashed. On Sviatogor's back was a crystal box, shining with light. He stopped in a mountain plain and took off the crystal box. Out walked the most beautiful woman Ilya had ever seen. Her eyes were like stars, and her hair was as gold as the sun itself. Sviatogor's wife pulled a great tablecloth from the saddlebag and began to prepare lunch, right there in the mountain plain. She turned toward Ilya, and happened to notice him. But she said nothing, so that Ilya wondered.

After a time, Sviatogor fell asleep, content with his food and the glories of the sunny day.

Sviatogor's wife beckoned to Ilya.

"Sviatogor is a great warrior, but a stern one," she said. "He brooks no opposition, and since the days that Mother Rus no longer bears him, he envies the bogatyrs of the plains."

"But I have come here to learn from the great Sviatogor," Ilya persisted.

She shook her head, but said, "Very well. Climb into his pocket, young warrior, you and your horse. When the time is right, you will know what to do."

Sometime later, Sviatogor woke up.

"Come, my dear, let us be on our way," he said.

"Sviatogor," said his wife. "I am tired of being in that crystal box. I will remain here for a time. You go on and come back for me in the evening."

And so he did.

But his great horse hardly bore him more than a few minutes when it began to trip under him.

"You bag of grass!" bellowed Sviatogor. "How is it you cannot ride in a straight line?"

His horse turned to him and spoke in a human voice.

"Sviatogor! I've always borne you and your wife. But now I have to bear two warriors, and a warrior horse to boot!"

Surprised, Sviatogor reached into his pocket, and was surprised to find a warrior and a warrior horse.

"Where are you from, brave youngster? What name and place do you hark from?"

"My name is Ilya Muromets, Ivan's son, I wanted to see the great Sviatogor for myself, for it is said that no longer does he ride on Mother Rus's lands, no longer does he come to teach us youngsters the art of war."

The great warrior answered him, "I would gladly ride on dear Mother Rus, but she no longer bears me. I am not allowed to ride to Holy Rus, but only to walk the peaks here in the north. Come, ride with me on the peaks, on these holy ridges and mounts."

And they did, riding together and learning much from each other. And they became friends of the heart, even exchanging the crosses that each wore on his chest.

Sviatogor spoke as they rode through that wild country.

"Tell me, Ilya, is the strength in your arms great or small?"

Ilya answered, "It is not great, Sviatogor. I am only a stripling still."

Sviatogor boasted, "Well, then. Hear what kind of strength I have. If there were a pillar in the bones of earth, as wide as the earth itself, reaching all the way to heaven, and if in that pillar there were a golden ring, I would flip the entire earth upside down."

And so they rode for a long time.

One day, as they rode together in brotherly converse, they saw a wondrous thing. A giant coffin of stone lay in the cliffs, its cover lying akimbo by its side.

"Come, Ilya Muromets," said Sviatogor the great, "Come, lie down in the coffin."

"No, Sviatogor," said Ilya, " 'tis a dangerous thing to do, to lie in a coffin before your time."

"Come, my friend! Surely you are no coward."

Ilya lay down in the coffin, but it was far too big for him.

"Here," said Sviatogor the great, "Let me try it on for size."

And he did. It was just the right size for the mountainous warrior.

"Come, brother of my heart, cover me with the coffin's cover!"

"No, Sviatogor," said Ilya, "this is nothing to jest with. What sort of a joke is it to bury yourself alive?"

Sviatogor, no longer laughing, took the cover himself and thrust it on top of the coffin, with him still inside. Suddenly, wonder of wonders! The cover and the coffin grew together into a single piece of unbroken stone.

Sviatogor the great pushed against the stone, tore at it, straining at his great arms. But all for nothing.

"Ilyusha! Get me out," he cried.

Ilya pushed, he pulled, he broke his fingers on the stone, he ripped his knees trying to pry the lid off the coffin.

"My brother, Ilya Muromets!" cried Sviatogor. "Take my great sword, the work of Krasnoiar himself, and hew apart the stone!"

"How can I do that, Sviatogor? I cannot even lift your mighty sword."

"Lean down closer to me," said Sviatogor, "and I will breathe some of my bogatyr-might into your lungs."

There was a tiny crack in the stone, and Sviatogor breathed into it. Ilya felt the strength double in his bones, in his mighty body.

He lifted the sword and swung it as hard as he could. The cliffs shook, the stones around them ground to powder. But in every place that the sword struck the coffin, a metal band appeared, holding the lid fast.

"Lean down closer to me," said Sviatogor, "I will breathe even more of my bogatyr-might into your lungs."

Sviatogor breathed into the crack. Ilya felt the strength in him quadruple. And he struck at the coffin lengthwise. The cliffs shook, the mountains bent like tree-trunks. But in every place that Ilya struck the coffin, a metal band held the lid ever faster.

"Lean down closer to me," said Sviatogor a third time, "I will breathe into you all the rest of my bogatyr-might."

"No, Sviatogor," said Ilya Muromets. "I don't need that strength. Or my bones will no longer be borne by Mother Rus herself."

Sviatogor lay there, silent for a time. Then he answered, "You are wise, Ilya Muromets. For if I had breathed my last breath into you, you would have been struck dead, and with me you would you have lain here for all time. And now, farewell, my little brother. Take my sword, for you alone can bear the work of Krasnoiar the great smith. As for my horse, leave it here with me. Tie it to my tomb. No one can manage her, except for me."

And Sviatogor, the greatest warrior Rus had ever known, fell silent for the final time.

Ilya Muromets, leaning on the great sword of Sviatogor, stood there. He didn't want to move. He didn't want to speak. Perhaps his elder brother would whisper a final parting, a final word of wisdom, a final blessing? Three days and three nights Ilya Muromets stood there. But Sviatogor said not a word.

The next morning, wiping away tears, Ilya Muromets put

on Sviatogor's sword and left the holy mountains for all time. It was time for him to take his place along the borders of Mother Rus. It was time for the land to welcome her new protector, the younger brother of Sviatogor the great.

Ilya Muromets and Nightingale the Outlaw

⚜

When Ilya Muromets had left his hearth and home, he was little more than a peasant's son. Unrefined, uncultured, a barefooted booby.

But he came home a brave warrior, dressed in shining mail and sparkling greaves. His helm, all in gold, caught the gleam of the sun, at his elbow a mace swung to and fro, at his left side, the sword of Sviatogor the great, and his right hand gripped a spear made of a trunk of a birch.

He came home to his mother, his father, and he fell on his knees before them a third time.

"Let me go, my dear mother and father. Bless me now to be Russia's new guardian."

But his father grew angry; his mother wept.

"No, Ilyusha, we don't give you our blessing to go. Stay with us here, we are old and decrepit. Lead us both by our hands until death comes for us. Only then will we give you the blessing you seek."

But Ilya would not rest with these words of his folk.

"Was it for this that I went to the holy hills, to learn from the greatest? Was it for this that Sviatogor himself blew his dying breath of might into my lungs? Was it for this that he gave me his sword so great, so that it might molder in an attic while I sit in a parlor? Did my strength and my might grow for thirty years, as in a cocoon, so that I could hide behind my mother's skirt?"

And his father sighed, and his mother sighed. They bent over double, they cried a bit more. But no longer did they withhold their blessing from a son who had outgrown them.

Only seven days they begged of him, to remain with them for a final week of fading joy.

No sooner did the sun rise on the eighth morning than Ilya jumped up, put on his mail, dressed his horse in Krasnoiar's armor. He tested his mace, he twirled his spear, he sharpened Sviatogor's mighty sword. He put a new string on his bow, struck his warrior-shield, and it rang like a bell on Pascha night.

Now it wasn't a willow whose branches drooped to the river, nor the fallen leaves that carpet the forest in fall, but it was a son who fell before his father, a warrior before his mother, begging a final good word.

And this time, Ilya's father waxed generous with his words.

"God forgive you all the sins you may have committed, my son, both known or unknown in the doing. My blessing I bestow on all deeds of valor and virtue, but not a single evil deed will I bless. Serve valiantly your mother, our Rus, cherish the calling of the bogatyr. Never bow and scrape before a prince, nor raise yourself proudly over a peasant. Neither give way to the enemy, though it cost you your hide. Be a guardian and protector of the weak, the orphaned, the smallest children. Be the keeper of all the Orthodox people!"

Efrosinia Alexandrovna shed a final tear as her son rode through the town, to the goggling eyes of his fellow villagers. After all, they had not yet seen him ride in his full warrior garb.

It was only in the wide plain that Ilya's sorrow came to haunt him. He saw his mother's face, he felt her tears hot on his face, and he stopped at that moment to stand on the firm earth of his holy land.

"I swear," he said, "for the sake of my weeping mother, that I will not pull my sword from its sheath, that I will not come off my horse, that I will not string an arrow to my bow, that I will not even dismount, from this moment until I come to the great city of Kiev."

Soon Ilya came to a parting of the ways. From one road, three branched out in different directions. At the center, at the parting, stood a waystone. On it, etched in white, were the following words:

"All three roads lead to Kiev. The straight rode will take the rider seven days. But it has fallen to disrepair. Thirty years it will take the rider now. The other two roads will take the rider two years."

Ilya rode straight.

Soon the road entered a dark wood and seemed to disappear in black mud and green, festering bogs. Ilya's horse could barely take a step without tripping or getting stuck fast.

Ilya sat on his horse and wondered. After all, he had promised his mother that he would not get off his horse until he reached Kiev, the great city. But if he didn't get off his horse, they would never make it.

"Forgive me, mother dearest! I made a promise to you, I did. But not for some fancy do I dismount now. I only do it in the greatest need."

And he got off his horse and led it by the bridle as he uprooted trees and tossed them across the worst of the boggy bits. He even built a few bridges while he was at it. And soon he had gotten through the swamp and found himself within shouting distance of Chernigov.

That beautiful city, though, was shut tight. For all around it a host of enemies seethed and swirled. Already they had scaling-ladders prepared, already their arrows were being covered with fiery pitch, already they had felled trees to break the gates down.

Ilya sat on his horse and wondered. After all, he had promised his mother that he would not shed blood, that he would not unsheathe his sword, until he came to Kiev, the great city.

"Forgive me, mother dearest! I made a promise to you, I did. But not for some fancy do I unsheathe my great sword now. But I do it for the children of Chernigov."

And Ilya Muromets fell on that host like a bolt of lightning.

Soon the host was nothing more than a mound of bodies piled as high as the white wall of Chernigov.

Then Ilya pushed the great gates open and walked into the city. It was as quiet as the grave.

At the top of a hill, inside the great city, Ilya saw a church with white walls and golden domes. He hastened to enter it, even as the sun began to set on that once-besieged city. The church was packed full of men armed, but white-faced. The priest served at the altar, and they all bowed their heads in frightened prayer.

Ilya stood through the service, crossing himself as the rites demanded. But he couldn't wait for it to end before he raised his voice to the congregation.

"Oh men of Chernigov, you cowards! To pray before battle is good, but better it would have been to let your swords and maces do the praying for you. Look! Your enemies are vanquished, even as you languish here behind the doors of the church."

And the wonder of Chernigov was very great as they saw the mound of the fallen.

"Stay with us, Ilya Muromets," they said to him. "Gold we will give you, silver as much as you like. Only be our war-leader, stay with us and protect us." And as they said this, they brought him three great goblets of gold, encrusted with jewels.

"Fie on you," answered Ilya Muromets. "I need none of your silver, not an ounce of your gold. It would be a great dishonor for me to remain among you, for my calling is to go to great Kiev."

"But you cannot go to Kiev," they retorted. "Have you not heard? There is but one road to the capital city. But at the outflow of the river Pochai, Nightingale the Outlaw, son of Rakhmat, has made his nest of thievery. On seven oaks does he sit, on forty stumps. Forty warrior-sons he has to do his bidding, and his daughter Marya Soloviovnina is the worst of the lot. Do not go to Kiev, the great city, for surely you will perish on the way."

"I may as well return to hide behind my mother's skirts if I should listen to your words," said Ilya.

And he rode on toward Kiev as the sun set.

The next morning, as the dust rose to meet the sun, Ilya approached the vile nest of Nightingale the Outlaw, son of Rakhmat, sitting on his seven oaks, his forty stumps. Nightingale saw the coming of the warrior, and he laughed.

"Here comes another one," he said to himself.

Nightingale began to whistle like a bird, to growl like a beast, to hiss like a snake. At the force of that sound, the trees bowed down to the earth itself, a wind rushed, pinning even the beasts in the field down to the earth. Ilya Muromets sat on his horse, as though nailed to the ground. But soon even his great warrior-horse fell to one knee.

"Why, you bag of grass, you useless fodder for wolves! Why did I raise you, why did I feed you, if you would bow down at the first sign of danger?"

And Ilya sat on his horse, and he wondered, even in the midst of the roaring, the whistling, and the hissing. After all, he promised his mother that he would not put an arrow to the bowstring until he came to Kiev, the great city.

"Forgive me, mother dearest! I made a promise to you, I

did. But not for some fancy do I set my arrow to the bowstring. I do it for the all the people of Rus."

Then he pulled his bowstring all the way to his right ear.

"Fly, my arrow, fly true. Pierce into Nightingale's right eye, and come out his left nostril. Go now, and serve me well."

And the arrow flew straight, and it pierced Nightingale's right eye, and it came out his left nostril.

Nightingale fell, silent, to the bare earth. Ilya took him and chained him to the saddle of his great war-horse. Then he rode on, on, toward the great city of Kiev.

As he rode, the forty sons of Nightingale, son of Rakhmat, saw in the distance the dust of a rider approaching them.

"Look, Mother," they said as one. "Our father the outlaw is bringing back another foolish peasant-warrior of the pathetic Rus, chained to his saddle bags!"

But the wife of Nightingale, Akulina Schelkanovna, had eyes like a hawk. She saw how it truly was.

"No, my sons. It is the other way around. It is your father who is chained to the saddle. Hurry now, grab your weapons, save your father from that foolish warrior."

And they did. All forty of them, bristling and armed to the teeth, rushed at Ilya Mumorets on their horses of the plains.

But as they approached, Nightingale himself called out to them.

"No, my sons. Don't attack this good warrior of the Rus. Gather all the gold we have, all the silver and mother-of-pearl. Buy back my freedom, for you are no match for this great man."

Then the sons of Nightingale, the wind no longer in their sails, rushed to gather the greatest ransom the world has ever seen.

But Marya Soloviovnina, the daughter-warrior of Nightingale, would have none of it. She took the metal bar from their gates, three hundred pounds and more it was, and she struck Ilya Muromets right between the ears.

That blow rung in Ilya's head like a bell clanging during a village-fire. And then, Ilya Muromets got angry.

He picked up Marya Soloviovnina like she was a sheaf of wheat and threw her. She flew like a bird, until she landed head first in the ground, losing her wits completely. When she came back to consciousness, she shook her head, which felt like all the bees in the world had come to make a home of it.

"Oh, what possessed me," she said, "to tease such a warrior?"

But Ilya had no time for her. He broke into the holds and keeps of the outlaw family. There, behind walls and bars and screens and chains as thick as a man's hand, he found ninety-nine warriors imprisoned.

"Get up, lazybones!" he jeered at them. "Haven't you heard? There's an outlaw on the road to Kiev."

Then Ilya rode to the capital city, Nightingale still chained to his saddle. He didn't bother to knock at the gates. He didn't bother to call the door-wardens. He whispered in his horse's ear, and it jumped clear of the walls of the city, landing in the city square, right at the foot of Vladimir the Prince's own palace.

Ilya Muromets dismounted and did the proper thing: he crossed himself in four directions, then he bowed deeply to the ground. A fifth time he crossed himself, but that was for the health and life of Vladimir the beautiful sun himself.

Into the hall of feasting Ilya went, waiting for no man to introduce him or to allow him in.

"Good morning to you, dear Vladimir, prince, the beautiful sun of this holy land."

At that greeting, all the boyars seethed like a pack of dogs.

"What is this barefooted booby of a peasant? How dare he come here with no one to announce him, all the way to the feet of Vladimir the prince!"

But Vladimir kept his peace and asked the young warrior,

"Tell me, young man, who are you and of what tribe? Are you come to us from a foreign land?"

"I am of this holy land, O Prince," said Ilya. "From Murom I come, from the village of Karacharovo. My father is a peasant of the land, Ivan his name. My own is Ilya Muromets! Just yesterday I stood at vigil in the church of Chernigov, and today for liturgy I have come to Kiev, the great city."

Again the boyars seethed and cackled like a pack of jackals.

"Listen to him, that barefooted booby of a peasant. Cast him out, O prince, as a raving liar. For what man can stand at vigil in Chernigov? You know yourself that enemies besiege it all around."

Ilya said to them, growing in anger. "You know of the enemies, and yet you sit here and drink? Yes, Chernigov was surrounded on all sides. But I hacked them with my sword, I stomped them with my horse, and the rest I bound in chains."

Again the boyars seethed and cackled like a pack of barking dogs.

"Listen to him, that barefooted booby of a peasant. Cast him out, O prince, as a raving liar. He has not defeated an army near Chernigov. And what's more, he's too stupid to know that Kiev itself is unreachable. For the roads are ruled by the outlaw Nightingale and his forty warrior sons."

At that, Ilya turned away from the boyars, ignoring them.

"As for that, Vladimir, prince and sun of this holy land, I have captured the Nightingale, and he is here even now, chained to my saddle."

The court rose in uproar, the prince first of all.

"Oh, Ilya Muromets, you marvel! Show me, show me the man who has brought so much grief to my lands."

And they all tumbled down the stairs to the courtyard, where Ilya's warrior horse still stood, bearing the chained Nightingale like a bag of fodder.

"Nightingale, you outlaw," said Vladimir the prince, "will

you do me a service? I would like to hear you whistle like a bird, roar like a beast, hiss like a snake for myself."

But the outlaw turned from the prince and said, "I do nothing but the bidding of Ilya Muromets."

Vladimir begged Ilya to let him hear the Nightingale's famous song.

" I cannot," protested the outlaw, "for my throat is parched and my lips are sealed with blood."

Ilya brought him a bucket of wine and let him drink. "Only take care," he said to the outlaw, "Only a half-whistle, only a half-roar, only a half-hiss. That's all you're allowed to do."

But the outlaw felt the wine coursing through his body like hot blood in his veins. And he thought this was the chance that he needed.

So he whistled as he had never whistled before. He roared as he had never roared. He hissed as he had never hissed.

The buildings shook, the bell towers swayed, the boyars groveled, and even Vladimir himself crawled on the ground from the blast of Nightingale's song.

"Ilya Muromets," the prince begged, barely speaking. "I have had my fill of this song."

Ilya Muromets picked the outlaw up by his scruff. He threw him up to the sky. The clouds themselves parted as the outlaw flew up, then fell back down to Mother Earth. To the shoulders he was buried under the dirt. And that was the end of Nightingale's song.

"Come, Ilya Muromets," said Vladimir the prince, as the boyars still groveled, afraid to stand up. "Come and sit in the war-leader's chair. It is yours if you want it."

And Ilya went up with the prince, and he sat in the great hall of feasting. And from that day on, he became war-leader of the armies of the capital city.

Volga the Warrior Mage

꧁꧂

The sun set behind the trees, beyond the wide blue sea. The sky was sowed with stars in the midst of darkness. Among the seeds, the moon shone bright. Just like that moon one evening was born a new bogatyr in Kiev, young Volga Vseslav'evich. At his birth, Mother Earth herself shuddered, the distant land of India shook, the blue sea-ocean quaked in fear at the birth of that mighty child, young Volga Vseslav'evich.

The fish plumbed the depths of ocean, the birds flew to the heights of heaven, the rams and the deer jumped over the mountains, the beasts of the forest sought their holes in the ground, even the wolves, the bears, the weasels and the marmots hurried deep to their holes in the earth.

Only an hour and a half after his mother gave birth, young Volga Vseslav'evich spoke, and it was light thunder.

"Greeting my mother, my darling mother. Stop wrapping me in swaddling clothes. Stop tying me up with silken ties, I need a different kind of swaddle now. Get me mail and greaves and a helm for my head! Not a cap, not a hat, but a hundred-pound helm. Put a mace in my right hand, a whip in my left, at my feet lay a spear and a saddle to boot!

Five years old was young Volga Vseslav'evich. Mother Earth shook again at the sight of the stripling, the beasts in the forests ran away in fear, the birds left their perches for heaven. Seven years he attained; it was time for his schooling. But no sooner he saw a book than he read it. No sooner a pen, than he wrote in fine script. Ten years passed from that glorious day of his birth, and already he knew the deep secrets of old.

The first wisdom he learned: how to turn into a falcon. The second wisdom he learned: how to turn into a wolf of the forest. The third wisdom he learned: how to turn into a ram with golden horns.

Then he turned all of twelve, and it was time to get to work. He gathered a war-band to follow his lead. A band of young people, no older than he, but braver and stronger than all. By the time he was fifteen, he had thirty men minus one. The thirtieth place he took for himself. And not one of them was older than Volga himself. A war band of warriors, all fifteen years old.

Then Volga spoke aloud to his warrior-friends.

"Hail, friends of my heart, warriors of renown. Listen to your elder brother. And do the deed that I command this day. Each of you build a trap of wood and silk, then go out into the deep forests. Let's see what kind of hunters you make; hunt for marmot and mink and hare.

For three days they hunted, for three nights they toiled. But not a single beast could any one of them catch.

Then Volga turned himself into a wolf of the glens. He leaped on the earth, flew through the tall trees, grabbing weasels and marmots and minks with a flash. Even rabbits and hares, even bears, badgers, wolves were not spared in the magical hunt.

Then he dressed his warriors in mink and badger, he fed them on rabbit meat, to their heart's content.

Then he said to his brothers a second time.

"Hail, friends of my heart, warriors of renown! Listen to

your elder brother. And do the deed that I command this day. Each of you build a fine net of silk. And catch the birds of the skies!"

For three days they hunted, for three days they toiled, but no goose, no sparrow, no swan did they catch.

So Volga turned himself into a falcon and flew all the way to the clouds, all the way to the deep, blue sea. As he flew, he struck down in his wake every goose, every swan, every bird he could find. Even ducks fell before him, not knowing what hit them.

And he fed his warriors for a week and a day, and they drank and ate to their heart's content.

Then Volga spoke aloud to his warrior-friends.

"Hail, friends of my heart, warriors of renown. Listen to your elder brother. And do the deed that I command this day. Build yourselves a wooden boat, go out to the waters to fish. Catch me pike, catch me salmon, whatever you find. And some sturgeon with roe to go with it."

They did as he said. For three days they fished, day and night in the colds of the sea. Not a single fish could they catch all that time.

So Volga turned himself into a pike and flew through the waves like a bird in the sky. Everywhere he went, the fish went flying from the waves right into the ready nets.

By that time Kiev-city was roiling with news. It was said that the king of India himself planned a war on the land of the Rus, so that he could sit in Vladimir's own throne, and burn the churches to the ground.

Then Volga spoke aloud to his warrior-friends.

"Tell me, friends of my heart, warriors of renown. There are thirty of you, minus one. Listen to the words your elder brother speaks. Is there any among you who knows how to turn into a ram? Any one who would travel to the distant Indian land, to listen in at the king's own window?"

And like a carpet of leaves in the fall, twenty-nine young warriors fell before him.

"There is none among us, Volga, our brother. Only you can do this thing that you ask."

And so Volga turned himself into a ram; in a single leap, he traveled half the way, and after the second, he was at the very gates. Then Volga Vseslav'evich turned into a sparrow, and he flew to sit at the king's own window. And he listened while the king himself, great Saltyk Stavrul'evich, spoke with his beautiful young wife.

He said, "Oh my queen, Azviakovna the Fair, what do you know of the world out there? I hear that in Rus the grass is growing a new way. The flowers are flowering differently. They say that Volga the warrior has died. It is time for me to attack those Rus, to take for myself nine cities, to give them to my nine sons, and for you, Azviakovna, a sable coat!"

"Listen to me, King Saltyk, my dear," said the lady, falling at his feet. "Here's what I know, and it's not what you've heard. The grass in Rus grows as it always has. The flowers are blooming as they have every year, and in a dream I had as I slept last night, I saw a field, and over that field, two birds flew toward each other. The first was a sparrow, the second a raven, but the sparrow attacked, and the raven fell, as the sparrow pecked its eyes out and pulled out its feathers. Don't you know? That sparrow is Volga himself, and the raven, that's you, King Saltyk!"

But the king would have none of it, and he let his wife have it. On a cheek he gave it to her, on the second, again, then he threw her to the ground in righteous anger.

"You would have me despoil my sons, all nine? Not to give them a gift of a city for each? Well, such a gift I will give them, but no coat will you get!"

And as she wept, he mumbled to himself, "What a queen you are, Azviakovna the Fair, to see such dreams for your lord and husband. The sable coat I will keep for myself."

And Volga wasted none of the time that remained. He turned into a wolf, right there in the court. And he ran to the stables and ate all the horses. Then he turned to a mink, to a sable, a weasel, and he ran to the armory to rip up all the bowstrings, to bend all the swords and to break all the maces. Then he turned into a falcon and flew up to the clouds until he flew to his friends, the war-band in waiting.

They slept, to a man, and he woke them up, saying,

"Hail, friends of my heart, warriors of renown to come. Is it time to sleep? No! It's time for glory. We're going to India to war."

They came to the white wall of the far Eastern city, but the city was walled with what seemed like a mountain. The stone was white, the windows were barred, and the gates were like teeth in the mouth of a bear.

Bristling on the walls were swords and spears, and the windows seethed with arrows nocked in bows.

"Oh Volga," moaned his war-band, their faces ashen in fear. "We have wasted a trip. How on earth can we fight, if that wall, like a mountain, stands between us and the king?"

But Volga was wise far beyond his tender years.

He turned himself into an ant, then did the same to his brothers. And they climbed the walls, both up and down again. And no one was the wiser.

Then as they stood at the gates of the palace, he turned them all back into warriors of Rus.

"Hail, friends of my heart, warriors of renown to be! Go, fight the men of the Indian king. But harm neither woman nor child."

And they did, as the wailing and mourning began, fighting wild like their brother the changeling.

But Volga himself ran up the palace's stairway, right up to the bedroom of Saltyk the great. The doors were of iron, bound up with hooks and bars. But Volga just kicked them down, to see India's pride cowering in a corner like a slave.

And Volga spoke to him, he cried aloud, "You kings don't get nearly enough education. It's time to be punished."

And he threw him against the floor, on the same spot where earlier, he had thrown his own wife to the bricks.

And the riches of that land were shared by Volga and his thirty great men minus one. But Volga for himself took a single prize. At his side on a horse rode Azviakovna the Fair. A princess to the Rus she would be.

Dobrynia Nikitich and the Dragon

❧

When Ilya Muromets became the war-leader for Kiev, the great city, he was greeted by two of Prince Vladimir's finest. But one of them, Alyosha the priest's son, was angry. In the middle of the feast, he threw down his goblet, and the wine fell on the marble floors like blood.

"I protest, fair prince," said the priest's son. He was young and hasty and a little too full of himself. He couldn't help it, poor lad. The ladies were wild for him.

"How can you give the war-leader's chair, which stood so long empty, to this peasant's whelp with no name? You dishonor this hall, these fair knights, your own name!"

But just as Vladimir was about to explode and call for the head of the son of the priest, the other of the two bogatyrs, Dobrynia Nikitich, stood up in the breach in defense of his own.

"Alyosha, calm down. This way is beneath you. Or do you believe you know better than all? This Ilya, he has proven himself to be hale, and worthy. To the credit of this court, the prince values courage over blood. Let's wait and see how our leader leads. If we is unworthy, his own actions will down him."

And Alyosha subsided and bowed to Ilya.

But how did Dobrynia become such a wise one?
It's time for his tale to be told.

When he was still young, Dobrynia Nikitich lost his own father. All he had was his mother. And his mother, well, a widow must care for who's left. So she fussed and she coddled, to Dobrynia's disgust.

One day, she told him, insisting, cajoling.

"Dobrynia, my love. Don't you ride to the fields, don't you climb those tall mountains, and don't trample the serpents. I know you've been hearing the rumors. The slaves of the Rus have it bad in their bondage. But the serpents, they're evil! And don't come to Puchai, the river, for it's wild as a beast. Don't swim in the streams, or haven't you heard? There's fire in those waves, they'll burn you to a crisp!"

But Dobrynia didn't listen, and at once he got up and saddled his warhorse, and off he rode. Into the fields, up to the high mountains, and with his horse-hooves he trampled the serpents, the children of the wyrm, and he released all their slaves.

It's hard work to go stamping the seed of the devil. His heart and his body were sore and hot, so he rode with his horse to the cursed shore of Puchai. He jumped off (he was young still then) and he took off his chain mail, his greaves, his sword, and all of his arms.

He jumped into the first stream, he plunged into the second. And to himself, out loud, he said these words:

"Was it to me, to Dobrynia, that my mother was speaking? Me, Nikitich, that she cajoled and fussed over, telling me not to ride into other fields, not to climb the tall mountains? Not to save the slaves nor to swim in Puchai? For wild as a beast, they say, are her waves. And the second of three streams burns like fire. But look, Puchai is a lamb and a babe. It's a puddle left over from summer showers."

Hardly had he finished than a wind came from nowhere. No, not a wind, but a cloud rushing over him, windless, booming with thunder, but no flashes of lightning. Instead of those sparks, a great dragon alighted with three heads. Zmei Gorynich the monster, no longer a legend, but a beast with red eyes: all six on Dobrynia.

And the accursed wyrm spoke aloud to the warrior:

"Now you're mine, Dobrynia, in my clutches, my claws. If I want, Dobrynia, I'll drown you right now. If I want, Dobrynia, my jaws will dismember you. If I want, Dobrynia, I'll eat you for lunch, or maybe I'll take you to the caves of my home. To season you, to butter you up for my children to snack on."

And with no further words, the dragon struck. But Dobrynia was a swimmer no less than a swordsman. He dove underwater, and came up at the shore. However, no horse could he find—it had fled or been eaten. And no mail, no arms, not even a shirt. All he found was a hat from the lands of the Greeks, a pilgrim's headdress. He filled it with sand, and he hurled it at the dragon. A single head came flying off a single neck. Two left to go.

The dragon fell, more in shock than in pain, but Dobrynia was quick on his feet, and he pounced. On his cross-chain Dobrynia had a two-edged knife, and he lunged at the white, soft chest of the beast.

But Zmei Gorynich exclaimed,

"Oh you great warrior, Dobrynia, son of Nikita! Let us make a bargain together, you and I, a great commandment, never to be broken. May you never set foot on the plain or the hills, may you never again kill my children, and I will refrain from my flights to your land. I will cease to maraud and to take any slaves; I will only eat goats and rams in the hills.

Then Dobrynia got up and released the foul snake. And Zmei flew away to the skies. At once, the dragon flew back toward Kiev, and he saw the prince's niece walking below. The young Zabava Potiatichna, walking with her maids on the roads of that town.

Then the dragon descended to the earth and the cobbles, he seized the princess and flew back to the hills.

For three days, Vladimir, the sun of his people, for three days he rang the bells of alarm, and he called to his court all the bogatyri of old.

"Who will ride to the fields, who will climb the high mountains, who will rescue my niece, young Zabava Potiatichna?

Then Alyosha the son of the priest piped up.

"Oh Vladimir, you sun of your people. There's only one knight who can help in your woe. Haven't you heard? Dobrynia made a pact with the wyrm. It promised him never to fly over Rus, and he gave his word to avoid the high mountains.

"Well, the beast broke his word, so the same must he do. And the dragon will be forced to give her up without a fight."

Cunning was Alyosha, and not always so brave as some of the prince's court, but his words won Vladimir, and he turned to Dobrynia, and spoke from the throne.

"On you I lay this charge, my friend. Ride to the fields, climb the high mountains. Bring back my princess, my niece Zabava. If you don't, then it's off with your head, I'm afraid."

Dobrynia went home, and he wept as he walked. His mother came out, Ofimia Alexandrovna, sensing his grief, and she said,

"Hail, my warrior, son of my body, good Dobrynia Nikitich. Why do you weep, was the feast not to your liking? Did someone take your place at the table? Or did a fool use your head as the butt of a joke?"

And Dobrynia the strong answered her,

"Hail, mother, you honored widow, Ofimia Alexandrovna! All the places were proper, the wine was the best. No fool dared to make me the butt of his joke. But Vladimir himself, bright sun of his people, he laid on my head a terrible deed. To the plains I must go, to climb the high mountains, to dig to the caves of Gorynich himself. For Zmei has broken his devilish word, and he stole Zabava Potiatichna."

Then the widow herself, Ofimia Alexandrovna, spoke wisely for once, and counseled her son. "Go to bed, my fair warrior, early to rise. May the light of the sun give you wisdom. The morning is wiser than the evening, you know."

And he did. Getting up with the sun in the morning, he washed himself white, and dressed in his finest. He chose his best horse and he saddled it with gold. He took his best sword and his heaviest mail. And twelve times he knotted the saddle to his horse. A thirteenth time for good measure he tied it, lest the horse lose the rider in flight.

As he rode to the plains, his mother came out to him. In her hands she held a fine whip made of silk.

"When you go the plains, to the mountains you ride, when you trample the snakelings and free all the slaves, there'll come a time when Burka, your favorite, will tire from the stamping and will try to go home.

"When that happens, you strike her between her legs, between her ears, between her back sides, and Burushka will jump and stamp even more. Only then will you kill all the snakelings."

And so he did. As soon as he climbed the high mountains, the ground rippled and seethed with snakes. And Burka stamped like her life depended on it, until she began to flag and to tire. And so Dobrynia struck her as his mother had told him, and his horse jumped all the higher, until the snakelings lay dead in an ocean of blood.

Then Zmei himself slithered out of his caves, and said, "Hail, Dobrynia, you oathbreaker! Why did you come here? Why did you trample my children again?"

And Dobrynia spoke up, "You accursed dragon-devil! Why did you fly home over Kiev the great city? Why did you take the prince's own blood? You are oathbreaker first, but I'm willing to talk. Give Zabava to me, and your hide will be safe."

But Zmei Gorynich didn't answer, he just flew into battle. And the bogatyr and the dragon fought and fought. For three days they tore at each other and struck and mauled. But Dobrynia couldn't kill the foul beast.

At last, his heart failed him, and he looked for an exit. But then, a voice from the heavens exclaimed,

"Three days you battled, my warrior fair! Hold on! Three more hours, and victory is yours."

He did, and in three hours, he hacked the wyrm down, but the blood poured out like an ocean of red. And Dobrynia wanted to run from that flood, but again, a voice from the heavens exclaimed,

"Three days you battled, in three hours you prevailed. Remain three more hours amid this ocean of blood, then take your spear and strike the hard earth.

When you do, say aloud, "Open wide, Mother Earth, open up to all four of your quarters. Drink the blood of the beast, let it flow into you."

And earth opened up and it drank.

Then Dobrynia descended to the foul-smelling lair, there he found forty kings, forty princes, and a countless host of armed soldiers to boot.

Then Dobrynia, he spoke to those men in the caves, "Go back home to your lands, leave the Rus in your wake, as for you, Zabava Potiatichna, for you I have come, for you I have fought. It is time to go back to the city."

Nikita the Tanner

❧❧❧

The river Dniepr is a river of gold, for the sun itself comes to her shores to play there. And why shouldn't it? For the sun of his people, Vladimir the great, lives there in his city of hills, glorious Kiev of the Rus. Well-known was that city for its warriors of old, for the bogatyri, led by Ilya Muromets and Dobrynia son of Nikita. But in even older days, when Vladimir was young, the bogatyri had not yet found their name.

Instead, the city was known for the beauty of its daughters. Often on a spring morning they would gather the flowers of the field and make crowns of them, plaiting them while singing, wearing them in song, and dancing in song to the banks of Dniepr the great. The whole city, nay, the countryside itself, with its wild creatures would stop and look at the train of beauties with their crowns that made the sun itself red with envy.

Those were happy days. Days of no worries.

Days that could not possibly last forever.

One day, Kiev was struck with a force of evil like a sudden thunderstorm in the summer.

A certain dragon—green scaled, red-eyed, and black-hearted—took to coming to Kiev to pass the time. With all six of his eyes like bores in three heads, the beast looked on the beauties of Kiev and wanted them with all the dragon lust he usually reserved for hoards of gold.

The coming of that beast was like the darkening of the sun in the middle of the day, and terribly he cried at the cowering hordes:

"You see your fine city of domes and hills? Not a stone on a stone will remain there once I'm through with it. With fire from my belly I'll scorch you to ash. But if you prefer to remain whole and living, then a tax I'll insist on. Once a month I will come to the shores of the Dniepr. Once a month, you must give me a daughter of yours. A fitting sacrifice for me to feast on.

The Kievans wept, the city-dwellers cried. Of course, they felt sorry for the beauties, their daughters. But they preferred their lives even more.

And so, once a month, lots were drawn in the city. Once a month, a household erupted in wails. Once a month, a beauty of Kiev was given as sacrifice to the demon of fire.

And so it went for months upon months. Until lo! No more daughters were left. Only Vladimir's own, the princess herself, had avoided the lots for months upon months.

But what could Vladimir do? He dressed her in gold, in silk, and brocade, and he chained her to an oak on the banks of the Dniepr. All alone she was left, except for her dove. A bird of the skies as her only friend.

There she stood, the princess of Rus. She was afraid, of course, but she refused to show it. A king's daughter she was after all. But then she heard the noise. Wings, wings the size of a house, each beat a gust of a blizzard.

And the dragon alighted before her, its three heads weaving back and forth in an unholy dance.

But the beast didn't scorch her, the dragon didn't eat her. It sat there, entranced, all six eyes on her form, till she thought she would melt from the heat of that gaze.

No, the dragon had other intentions for her.

"I won't eat you," he said, "you're too good for that fate. I will take you to my lair, there to cook and clean. Be a wife to me, lady, and I'll keep you alive."

And he grabbed Vladimir's daughter and flew.

They flew for what seemed a year and a day. Over mountains and lakes, over forests so thick that they looked like the hide of an earth-sized beast. And there, in the midst of that endless wood, he alighted. A cave yawned in a black rock, and inside was a stench of aeons of death.

"Here's my home, little wife. Enjoy your stay."

And he left once again to his hunting and gorging.

The princess remained, but she wasn't alone. The dove was there, always near her.

During the day, she remained in the cave. By the evening the dragon returned with its catch. It would eat in a corner and stare at the princess, saying nothing, but munching on bones and on flesh.

One morning, as soon as the snake flew away, the princess turned to her dove and she said,

"Fly home, little bird, bear this letter to Papa. To Vladimir the sun of his people, to his wife. Perhaps they will think of some way for me to escape?"

And the dove flew all day and all evening without rest. By the morning, the domes of the city in sight, it flew through the window to the feet of the prince.

And Vladimir rejoiced, for he thought his daughter was dead.

That day they assembled all the greatest of the land.

"Tell me, friends," said Vladimir, "what to do? How to act? Can we save our dear princess from the clutches of the worm?"

And the wise of the city came back with this answer.

"Write a letter to your daughter. Have her speak to the beast. Use her wiles to find if he has any weakness."

And so he did.

One evening, the dragon returned to his home. He was hungry, he was grumpy, for nothing could he catch. He almost caught a ram with golden horns, but it was too fast for him. Was he getting old? He wondered.

But the sight of the princess healed all tiredness for his bones. And then, Oh the joy! She actually spoke to him!

These were the words that she said to the wyrm:

"Tell me, zmeiushka-zmei, so mighty and strong. I can't imagine that anyone can be stronger than you."

And the dragon chuckled to himself at her words.

"So be it," he hissed. "You have pleased me so far, so I'll tell you a secret. There is no one stronger than I, save only one. A man, named Nikita, the tanner. He lives near the city. No one notices him, no one knows who he is. But a mightier man than he does not live. Him alone do I fear, he alone could defeat me."

And the dragon, content with his power and might, curled up to a ball, and fell asleep on the spot.

But the princess took to her letters, and wrote.

"Find me Nikita the tanner, the mighty man of Kiev. Only he can defeat the dragon and save me."

The king immediately sent to the outskirts, to the village where Nikita plied his trade in obscurity.

"Save the princess, Nikita, do a service to your prince!"

But Nikita only grunted, and tore twelve pelts in half.

And no matter what the king said, not matter how much he asked, Nikita would not go.

"No, he said. "I'm a humble man. I work and I ply my trade. What do I have to do with dragons? This is knights' work, not the work of a tanner."

So Vladimir gathered all the children of Kiev, all the orphans, all the rich, and the poor and the merchants. All the children they had, and together they went in procession to the doors of the tanner himself.

"Dear Nikita," they cried, "don't you know what will happen? The day is coming, the first of the month. No more beauties remain, so they'll offer us next as sacrifice to the demon of fire."

Only then did Nikita look up from his work. And a tear appeared on his face of stone.

"Don't cry, little children. I'll give it a shot."

So Nikita prepared for battle. He took ten thousand pounds of hemp, soaked it in sap, and wrapped himself in it. Like a set of scales on his hide it looked. Neither sword, nor spear, not tooth could go through it. A tree he took to be his shield. And in his right, he carried a mace.

And he went to the lair.

But as soon as the dragon could smell him from afar, he barricaded his lair with a hundred felled trees.

"Come out, dragon," called Nikita, "or I'll break your walls down!"

And he struck the logs with the mace till they cracked.

So the dragon prepared for the battle. His teeth he sharpened, but he didn't have time. For the logs were no match for Nikita, they all broke.

And the snake slithered out, hissing out of three maws, and he blew smoke and fire at the tanner. But the warrior stood as though he were in a bathhouse enjoying a steam. And then, his mace went to work. To the right he struck, and a head lopped off. To the left, and another came crunching down.

"Stop, warrior!" said the snake. "Let's make a bargain, you and I. I will promise to leave the great city alone. And you will never come here, just leave me the princess. And as proof of my word, let's plant a great furrow, a barrier between your lands and mine."

Nikita stood there for a while in thought. "Fine," he said, "As you wish." And he took the largest plow he could find, and before the dragon knew what was up, he had hitched him up like an ox or a donkey.

"Come on and pull, let's make this border a good one!"

And they did, till they reached the Caspian Sea.

"Well and good, Nikita," said the wyrm, panting. "Now for hearth and for home."

"Not so fast!" said the tanner. "What? We've forgotten the sea. Or I know you, you'll say that the merchants are crossing into waters that are yours."

So the snake, still hitched up, swam into the great water. But Nikita just waited until they were deep. Then he struck the third head off, and the dragon sank down, to the bottom of that blue Caspian sea.

Then Nikita came back, with the princess beside him. And crowds of people came bearing gifts of gold and silver.

But Nikita just growled.

"What do I need with finery? Gold and baubles? Just leave me to my leather and work."

And Nikita went home to his village, his hearth, and no more did the beast bother Kiev the great.

The Wedding of Dobrynia Nikitich

✦

And so Dobrynia Nikitich returned home victorious after his fight with the wyrm. He rode through the woods, through the dirt roads, barely visible. Until all at once he stumbled on a ridden track. Deep were those hoof prints, no doubt about it. Only one sort of person could leave prints like that.

"My soul, there's a warrior in these woods," he said to himself.

And he whipped poor old Burka beneath him.

Soon he rode into a forest clearing. There, resting beside a warrior horse, he saw a foreign knight. No one he had ever encountered before.

"Tell me, fellow warrior, what land are you from? Who is your father, your mother?"

But the foreign knight answered rudely, with a smirk, "If you'd like to test my mettle, old man, then pull out your mace, and have at it!"

And Dobrynia's fury flashed like lightning. He sped on his horse and brought his mace down like a hammer. But the blow glanced off, and the warrior didn't budge. And Dobrynia turned aside, like a ten-pound weakling.

Furious at himself, he saw an old oak in the distance.

Winding his arm, he struck the poor tree. And nothing was left of it but splinters.

"Well, at least I know that my power's still there," he said to himself as he turned.

Once again he called out to the foreign knight, "Tell me, warrior, who are you? Of what land or what horde? Who is your father, your mother?"

And again the warrior smiled and barked, "If you'd like to test me, old man, try again, I dare you!"

And Dobrynia's blood boiled in his veins. He rushed on his horse, and he swung his great mace. And again, as he struck, the warrior didn't budge, but Nikita himself nearly fell off his horse!

Disgusted with himself, he found an old willow, and struck it with all that he had. In a flash, that willow was powder and dust.

"Well, at least I know that my strength is still there!"

This time, Dobrynia jumped off his horse, and approached the strange knight on foot.

"Tell me, brave warrior, of what country, what land? Why hide you your father, your mother?"

But the warrior laughed and laughed in his face. Then the warrior took off his helmet.

And the hair on her head flowed down her shoulders. She was a woman, to Dobrynia's surprise.

"What a pity! I thought the warriors of Rus were strong. But your blow is like the bite of a mosquito."

Then the warrior picked Dobrynia up with his horse, and she stuck them both into her pocket.

She sat on her horse and rode off into the woods.

But soon, her horse started stumbling.

"Why you silly nag, you bag of grass! Why can't you ride like a proper horse?"

"What can I do?" complained the horse. "It's not every day that I have to bear two warriors, and a warrior horse to boot."

Then the warrior maid stopped and spoke aloud to herself.

"If he's an old bogatyr, I'll chop his head off. If he's a young bogatyr, I'll make him a slave. If I like how he looks, I'll take him as a husband. But if he's ugly, I'll put him between my two palms and smash him into a pancake."

Then she looked at young Dobrynia, and he seemed to her very fine indeed.

Then she recognized him, and she smiled wide.

"Dobyrniushka, my love, young Nikitich!"

But he recognized her not a bit.

"What a warrior maid you are, but who? I've never met your like in my life. How do you know me?"

"To Kiev I've been, there I've seen young Nikita in state. After all, I'm a daughter to Mikula Selianinovich! That great warrior that Mother Earth loves. I rode out into the fields to find my joy, to see if anyone else could defeat me in battle. Now listen, fair warrior, Dobrynia Nikitich. Will you have me for wife or not? If not, no offense, but I'll smash you to paste, and make a pancake out of a warrior."

"Oh you marvel, Nastassia Mikulishna! I will make for you a golden crown, and I'll walk with you under it to the altar."

And together they rode back to Kiev, the great city. And Dobrynia fell on his knees before his mother Afimia Aleksandrovna. He asked for her forgiveness, he asked for her blessing, and he called all his brothers together to feast. To church, for their wedding. Just one of his brothers he neglected to call. Aliosha, the priest's son, he was a jokester and a lady's man. Better to keep him at home, thought Dobrynia to himself.

And that wedding was brighter and finer than any that Kiev had seen for many a year.

Sukhman the Young Warrior

❧

A war band was riding, riding to Kiev, to Vladimir in Kiev for the love of a feast. The war band arrived, the prince was ecstatic, and with joy did the feast start its course. As the warriors sat and feasted in plenty, the prince himself walked up and down the tables.

And as he walked, he said to his warriors, "Why of all this cheerful crowd, are you, Sukhman, such a sad-faced one? Is there not enough food? Is there not enough drink? Is there nothing that you can be boastful about?"

"Lord Prince Vladimir, a thought grows inside me, how to give even more joy to this festive assembly. I will go and hunt for a white, pure swan. Not a trapped swan, not a wounded bird. I will catch her in my hands and give her to you without scratch."

"Oh, light of my eyes, Sukhman, you marvel! What a kindness you'd do me. I ask for no more. Yes, get me a swan, a living swan, in my hands before the coming of dawn."

Sukhman got up, and he left the feast. He rode and he rode in the wide open fields, he watched through the forests and glades all around. He crossed many rivers and rode round blue lakes, but no matter what he did, not a single swan could he find, not a living one, not even a dead one. He couldn't even find a duck or a goose.

And the young warrior said aloud to himself, "What a sorrow has come over me! What will I do? With what gift will I return to the hills and the domes of fair Kiev? No, I will not, I cannot return. I will go to the Dniepr, that great river, instead.

And so, the young warrior rode to the river. "O Dniepr the Great! Dniepr the mighty! Why are your waters so mixed up with sand? Why have your streams become muddy and foul?"

And Dniepr the great spoke aloud to Sukhman, "Hail, brave warrior, wondrous Sukhman! Don't look at me now, don't stand by my shores. Don't fear me as you wonder at my waters befouled. But look instead beyond my shores, there's a host of ten thousand times two, an enemy army. Where they came from, who knows? But they're known as the Tatars. Every morning they breach my fair waters with pontoons to cross their great host into Rus! But whatever they build by the light of the day, I, Great Dniepr, destroy by the night. Now you see why my waters are foul and besmirched, and my streams so sluggish and slow."

And Sukhman the great warrior forsook the hunt, forgot the game, abandoned the feast. Instead, he pulled out his great sword and his shield. And he rode on his charger to battle alone.

Flash! went his sword. Stomp! went his horse. Like a cliff amidst waves stood the warrior true. Enemy hosts broke apart on his shield, and his sword was a scythe among wheat. Imminent victory filled him with joy.

But Sukhman, Sukhman! Look behind you, my warrior! Behind that old oak, that twisted old tree, a Tatar archer secretly lurks. There's his bow, there's an arrow, look behind you, Sukhman! Cover your back with a shield!

But no, you didn't look, no, you didn't hide. You never suspected the danger that lurked behind the tree in the shadows. After all, no warrior remembers himself in the thick and the heat of the battle as it rages. In the snap of an eyelid, the archer loosed from a bow drawn tight, an arrow true. The arrow flew, it moaned as it flew, and it entered the right side of Sukhman the Great, and it came out of his left and kept going.

Sukhman, our hero, fell down from his horse, and the enemies stood like a thunderhead rising. A sea of swords rose up in a flash to strike down the fair warrior where he lay.

But the warrior looked up, and he rose from the earth. He pulled the green grass from its roots in the ground. He covered his wounds, he filled them with leaves, and his mind was on fire, and his soul was aflame, and he pulled out that traitorous oak with its roots, and he smote down his enemies like grain.

The branches broke, the leaves flew apart, the roots shattered on impact, and as Sukhman scythed, the enemies fell. Until finally the wounded one felled the last man. A field of bodies had he sown for his prince.

And so he got up, and he mounted his horse, and he rode to fair Kiev, the city of light.

But the prince saw not the wounds on Sukhman, and he said, "Well, have you done as you promised? Surely you bear in your arms a fair gift. An unbloodied swan, caught with your hands?"

"O sun of your people," began the fair warrior. "I had not the leisure for hunting today. No time for games, no taste for sport. For Dniepr herself was filled with a horde, a force that no one has seen, called the Tatars. And I struck them all down to the last man!"

But the boyars who simpered at table all day would hear none of the boasting of fair Sukhman. "O sun of your people, prince Vladimir the great, this youth is a liar, and straight to your face. He tried, he failed, and now he invents a new enemy for the Rus, called the Tatars, what shame!"

The prince, stung with anger, boiled with rage: "Take Sukhman to the prisons, to the pits under earth. To the darkness with nothing but bread and water. Let him learn what it costs to boast without truth in this haven of warriors true."

All the warriors averted their eyes in shame, but the boyars rejoiced in their cups.

Only Ilya, fair Muromets, dared to counter the prince, "Sun of your people, allow me a word. Sukhman is righteous, Sukhman is true, never a false word passed those lips of his. Let him go free, O prince, and let me see if his tale is true.

No sooner said than done. Ilya rode from the domes and the hills, to the fields near the Dniepr, which roiled and stank. There he saw the field of bodies uncounted, a host of enemies dead on the ground as far as his eye could see. Then Ilya took the oak with its branches of blood and rode like the wind to the city.

"Prince Vladimir, sun of your people," he said. "Here is the oak that defeated an enemy so great that no city could stand in their way. As for you, proud boyars, see for yourself, lift the oak, show yourselves equal to the task. There are enough of you there, stop drinking and rise!"

Then the boyars got up and rushed to the oak, each trying his luck and his strength. But no one could so much as budge the great tree, nor lift it a handbreadth from the ground. Then they let poor Sukhman out of prison into the sun, and they told him to lift the great tree. And Sukhman took the oak, and lifted it high, and threw it beyond Kiev's walls to the fields.

Vladimir was ashamed, though he covered it well, as he offered great Sukhman a gift.

"Now I know that you're true, dear Sukhman the strong. And hear now my word and receive now my gift. A city I'll give you, no two, even three! Take the lands and sow them to your heart's content.

But Sukhman would not look his prince in the eye. "No reward would you give me before, and now... it's too late for all your gifts."

Sukhman mounted his warrior-horse and rode far from Kiev, far from all shame.

Filled with sorrow he was, his soul was aflame, and his heart beat twice as fast as before. The blood ran hot through his warrior body, and the leaves and the grass fell out of his wounds. The blood flowed fast like the Dniepr from his side.

"Oh my wounds, my wounds, pour out like a river! And you, my dear horse, my only true friend, when I fall from you back, when I can hold you no longer, don't sorrow for me, don't stand over me, but ride away, be free, go where you wish. To the glades filled with grass, to the fields filled with clover. Graze there to your heart's content, my friend. Drink the waters of freedom from Sukhman the river."

Then the rivers of blood ran their course and stopped. And Sukhman the river flowed on and on. And so died fair Sukhman, the warrior true. Glory be to him from age to age!

Ilya Muromets Quarrels with Prince Vladimir

For his shameful acts, for his falsehoods, for his wrong accusation that led to the death of Sukhmann the young warrior, Ilya Muromets grew furious with his prince. He was filled with sorrow and woe, his face covered with a dark cloud of anger. As he walked back and forth on the streets of great Kiev, he thought black thoughts to himself.

"I will teach that princeling a lesson; I will turn the insult on the offender. I will turn my arrows to the churches, and I will knock down the crosses of gold. I will tear the gold scales from the domes!"

No sooner said than done. He shot his arrows true, and down fell the crosses of gold, and it rained golden scales on the streets of Kiev. And Ilya cried out in a loud voice for all to hear:

"Come out, you poor, you destitute! Go, take that gold and eat and drink your fill today!"

At that, Prince Vladimir grew dark in thought: "How can I make peace with my dear Ilya? Maybe I can call him to a feast in his name? But he won't listen to me. Should I send my daughter? But how bad that would look? I know. I'll send the peacemaker, Dobrynia Nikitich.

Dobrynia was old, Dobrynia was wise, a quiet man of effective words. He always knew how to speak to a man, to calm a warrior in his rage or his cups. And he went and found Ilya Muromets, and he made peace between him and the prince.

As Ilya approached, Vladimir ran to him, taking his hands and leading him in.

"Oh, you brave warrior, Ilya Muromets! Before your place was with peasants, I know. But now, sit down at the head of the table!"

And Vladimir did what he did best. He hosted a feast in his honor.

But no peace did Ilya enjoy from the court. Like the fetid bubbling of a swamp in the heat, the boyars mumbled and whispered to the prince.

"Oh, where has such a horror been seen before? Such a shame that we've never imagined. Did you ever think that a poor farmer's son would lord it over the great of this court? Take a look at your favorite, O sun of your people, he has no respect, not for us, nor for you. That ermine you gave him with your own two hands? Look, he wears it like rags, shrugged off on one shoulder, and that fur-lined hat, cocked to the side! Who of us, dear prince, would dare to dress likewise? To show such disrespect to your gifts?

"But if that's not enough, hear now what he did. He went to the alehouse last night until late, wrapped in your ermine like a rag for a beggar. And these were the words that we heard him say, 'Look at this ermine robe as I throw it on the ground. I will do the same to Vladimir tomorrow'!"

At these words, the thoughts of the prince began to boil. Vladimir, sun of his people, didn't bother to verify the words of his courtiers. Didn't bother to ask the good counsel of others. He didn't think, he didn't wait, but commanded on the spot that deep holes in the ground be dug, that caves of old be uncovered. And he told his guards to take Ilya Muromets, to throw him into the pits, and to lock him up.

But if that wasn't enough, he commanded them all to cover the pits with stones and sand, so that no light or no air would get in there again.

And Ilya was entombed alive by his prince. No surprise, as soon as it happened—the next morning, in fact—all the warriors of the Rus simply rode away. They wanted nothing to do with a prince who would do such a thing to the best of their ranks. And what do you think? All the enemies of Kiev rejoiced as they made dark plans.

For no more are there guardians holding the ways of Mother Rus, the holy land of old.

The evil dog, King Kalin himself, rose up in that time and found his strength. Together with him was a host without count of heathen warriors with no hearts. He harried the poor, he burned the farms, he put to the flame both city and church. And soon his host, as countless as ants, approached the great river herself. All around fair Kiev the lands are aflame, and bridges go flying across fair Dniepr. The sun is darkened by smoke and by omen.

Only now does Vladimir awaken. Only now does he weep, only now does he wonder.

"What have I done to deserve such a fate? Surely the Lord punishes me for my sins, for my madness, my foolishness, my pride. For alone I am, in Rus's plight, not a single warrior in my train. Where are you now, my bogatyri? Where are you, my warriors true?"

Only then did the prince's own daughter approach, as he moaned and he groaned in his sorrow, as he said in his last despair, "If only Ilya were still alive, Kalin would not plunder the churches and homesteads, and my people would not suffer, nor my city burn!"

And Liubava Vladimirovna fell down at his feet.

"Forgive me, my father, sun of your people, for not heeding your words, your commands. For I saved fair Ilya from a death underground. All these years I've been feeding him and giving him drink. I saved him from death, and he's still alive, in the pit, that tomb for the living."

And Vladimir the prince rejoiced at the news.

"God forgive you, my dear, for not listening to me. Let's go together and open the doors, let's call our fair Ilya out from the pits, from the holes, from the horrors underground."

On his knees the prince approached the opened door, begging forgiveness, wiping his face with dirt in shame.

"Hail to you, great warrior Ilya! Listen to the plea of your prince, your tormentor. Come out to the light, I have news for you."

"Why have you come, O prince? Why do you visit me after so many years? Surely there's some dragon about or a host of enemies for me to kill for you. As soon as you need old Ilya, you call. Well, enough! I prefer the darkness these days."

"O Ilya, you fair warrior, great man of the Rus. Forgive me I beg you, my sins and my pride. It was madness, I say, not my own good sense. The bug-eyed boyars, they lied and they slandered. Come, sit on your warrior horse, go and ride, fair warrior, into the wide fields. Come and see the seething force of Kalin the dog, they're approaching, they're at the gates of our city! Come again, my dear warrior, stand for your people, for your fatherland, and forgive and protect even me, a sinner. If not me, then have mercy on Liubava, protect her from what is to come."

But Ilya Muromets gave his answer again, "I don't want any part of you, sun of your people. I won't fight for you, I won't serve you again. How many times have I entered the fray for this city of ingrates and boors? I am old, I am weak, I am blind like a mole. I prefer the dark, not the light."

And Liubava herself, with tears in her eyes, fell on her knees and crept into the pit.

"If only you'd come and see for yourself, what a terrible force is arrayed against us. What a heartless enemy stands at the gates, how they've orphaned the children, harassed the widows, and burned the homes of the poor that you love! They've stomped on the wheat, they've burned all the villages. So stand, Ilya Muromets, not for Vladimir, not for me, but stand, bogatyr for the widows, the children!"

And Ilyusha grew silent and thoughtful in the dark. He thought for an hour. He ruminated for two. And finally his face grew bright with decision. "I will stand, I will stand for holy Rus; I will stand for the abused, for the orphans and windows. I will smite that dog Kalin the king!"

And the old cossack, Ilya Muromets, rode on his horse once again after years of darkness. He rode to a hill to see the land, and he looked on all four sides of his country. Everywhere he looked, he saw nothing but seething hordes of enemies coming with fire. And his head, grayer than ever before, shook with wonder at such a sight.

"What a force has this dog, this King Kalin, called to his side in my absence! I could hardly ride around this army on my horse, not only I, but a wolf couldn't do it, nor a hawk in flight."

And Ilya Muromets, the warrior true, bowed the knee and prayed. He sat on his horse and rode at high speed, and he smote the Tatar host like a strike of lightning. Ilya's horse flies like a falcon on the hunt; Ilya sits astride like an eagle on a crag. Together they smite and they ride and they rout, he with spear, he with horse, he with mace and with sword, and his horse with its hooves like hammers of steel. Soon they cut a wide swath through the terrified Tatars, and he found himself at Kalin's own side.

His heart afire in his chest, he rose, and his horse reared up with him as he charged. Kalin the dog had no time to think, to plan, not even to flee. Like a strike of lightning, the mace struck him true, and he lost his sight in a flash. Ilya Muromets pierced the dog with his spear, and lifted him up for his soldiers to see. Then the Tatars roared with fear and with ire, but they fled before his wrath as he rode them down, striking them, stomping them, hacking and scything.

Kalin the dog's body he left in that field for the ravens, the wolves and the bears. And the warrior true came back to his city, to the court of Vladimir, sun of his people. But no one was there to meet him. They all cowered at home in their timorous fear.

As he walked to the palace, Ilya cried aloud, "Lie here on the ground, O spear of mine. I have no more strength to stick you into the earth. My hands are weak, they won't listen to me, my shoulders droop like an old, withered man's, my elbows are bent, my feet are in pain. I left my strength in the field today, for I fought without food, without drink. I defeated Kalin as a hungry man!"

The servants of the prince heard Ilya in the court, and they ran to tell what they heard.

"Prince Vladimir fair, sun of your people, though the sun rose in the morning, all it was cold, without clouds it was dim. But now, in the evening, though no sun is in the sky, it grows light again, warm and joyful. For Ilya Muromets is here, he's warmed us with his care, but no one has fed him in ages."

Then Vladimir himself ran to greet the bogatyr, and he took Ilya by the hand.

"I will gather the great of the Rus to a feast in your honor, Ilya. For a day, for two, for a week we will feast!"

But Ilya stood as still as stone.

"Hear me, O Prince, this Kalin, this dog, he's only the harbinger of things to come. There are larger berries than this still to ripen in the field of the dead and the fallen. Look for yourself to the east, to the setting sun. It's burning over there, that red sun of omen, and it tells of bloody days to come. It's not time for your feasts; it's not time for your wines. It's time to gather the bogatyri again, to call back all the warriors that your madness has cast out. For you, Vladimir, have lost them all, all the guardians of Rus the great."

The prince turned white with horror and shock. Full of despair, he cried out, "Go, my fair warrior, call them all back. Serve me this one final time. Call your brothers, tell them your tale, let the bogatyri stand again together for the glory of their faith and their fatherland."

Ilya Muromets and Batu Khan

❦

The horde of the enemy seethed and blustered. The heart-rending cries of the heathens make the souls of the Rus grow heavy and cold.

On a hill, on a mount, within sight of the domes of Kiev, that brightest of cities, Batu Khan, Batu's son, built a cloth-o-gold tent. There is stands, there it glistens in Rus's bright sun, a black mark, a dark omen of woe.

There he stood, Batu Khan, Batu's son, in the sun, and he cried to his hordes of Tatars: "Bring to me, you dogs, the best that you have. The fattest, the strongest, the one with sharp eyes, the one with keen ears, and a voice like a horn. And make sure that he speaks in the tongue of the Rus!"

His people went searching for this pride of the heathen. When they found him, they dressed him in silks and in satins, they put him on a horse and they led him to the hill. Batu Khan, Batu's son sent him thus to the city with a word from Batu to the prince of the Rus.

The doom-mouthed envoy rode into Kiev, not stopping till he reached the palace mount. Without waiting for entry, he pushed down the doors and rode, still mounted, into the hall of the feast. He trampled the tables that stood empty and bare, and he rode to the room with the throne. There his mud-shoed horse befouled the rugs, there his charger assaulted the boyars and guests, there the envoy dismounted, his boots on the tables, his rump on a chair in the presence of the king.

And he cried out like a horn, with his voice like a rattle:

"Hear the words, Vladimir, sun of these people,
Hear the words of Batu Khan Batu's son.
Clean out all the archers from your alleys and streets
Open wide all the halls of the boyars and princes
Clean up all the pavilions and the hall of feasting
Leave your churches for our horses, fitting stables for
     steeds,
And let your alleys and streets flow with wine and mead
Let the trestles groan from meat and from pie
So that every inch of this city of cities
Be bedecked with food for the Khan of the steppes.
Let Batu be the king of this finest of towns,
And Batu Khan, Batu's son will be gracious with you
And your head he will keep on your shoulders."

Vladimir heard, and Vladimir mourned, for he had no idea what to do. From Ilya he had heard not a word for a week, nor had any bogatyr returned to the city. And Vladimir sat at his table of oak, and he put a gold pen to paper. He wrote a letter to Batu Khan, Batu's son, a timorous dispatch, the words of a coward.

"O defeater of worlds, Lord Batu, Batu's son, I will clean out the alleys and street, I will open the doors to the halls and the feast-rooms, I will cover this city with trestles that bustle with food and with drink and with meat. In all things I will do your will."

This was the missive returned to Batu, which he read as he danced and he pranced and he sang, "There it is, there's your holy land of the great Rus! There's Vladimir the prince, my boot-licker!"

All this time Ilya Muromets rode on his horse in search of the lost warriors of Kiev. But he wasted much time, and he found no one at all, then he stumbled by chance on an ambush of Tatars. No small ambush was this, but the vanguard of Batu, which reached as far as the eye could see.

"How could the waters have borne such a tide of boats? How can Mother Earth herself bear their weight?" he asked. "Would that the caves of the earth opened up underneath and swallowed them all into her maw."

And from the stench of that horde of the heathen the sun itself grew pale and sick, the stars in the night sky faded and dimmed, and the mind, the soul grew weak, and the heart of man lost its joy.

And Ilya Muromets said to himself, "So be it. I will smite this host on my own."

And he charged them like a falcon in flight, he aroused his heart in his warrior chest, he drew his sword and his mace, and he reared with his horse as he rode.

Like a swirling storm Ilya Muromets charged straight at the black heart of Batu and his ranks. He scythed that horde like wheat and like grass, for three days and three night he battled without sleep, without food, without water, without rest.

Suddenly, his warrior horse began to speak with a human voice, "My master, brave warrior, Ilya Muromets of the Rus! This horde is too great, this power is too mighty. We alone can't prevail against Batu of the steppes. Let me go, Ilya Muromets, let me turn and flee, and we'll live to fight another day and night."

But Ilya barked angrily at his horse under him.

"You fodder for wolves, you bag of grass, what are you croaking down there like a raven without wings? Where is it

seen, or where is it heard that a bogatyr of the Rus left the
bloody fields? Never will they sing it of me!"

He beat his horse, and they entered the fray once again for
three days and three nights.

But then, Ilya's horse spoke a vatic word, his tongue
growing strong and oracular:

"Oh my master, brave warrior, Ilya of the Rus, no victory
awaits at the end of this day. For before you Batu has prepared
a great trick. He's dug three trenches in the fields ahead. If we
fall into the first, I will take you out. If we fall into the second,
I will raise you up, but that third one is deep. If we fall into it,
you will never see the sun's light again!"

But the old cossack warrior, Ilya Muromets the brave, had
no faith in the words of his warrior-horse.

"A horse you are not, nor a friend to me. You're a traitorous
dog in Batu-son's own pay."

And he plunged straight ahead into battle.

And it was as the horse had predicted. Through the first
trench they rode, and his horse pulled him out. The second
swallowed him, and his horse rose again. But the third was
deep, the third was profound, and its walls were of stone with
no purchase, no crack. And he fell with his horse, and with
him fell all Rus into the waiting hands of the dog Batu-khan.

As soon as he heard that Ilya had gone down, Batu-khan,
Batu's son called his soldiers to heel.

"Come together, my horde, it is time to attack. Kiev's
wines and its feasts are yours for the taking!"

Like waves against rocks, the horde crashed into Kiev.

The boyars quivered, the princes quaked, Vladimir himself
shut his door and wept.

And Kiev was left to the dogs at its walls.

But then, three old men appeared in the streets. They were
withered and bent from age and from cares. But their voices
were strong as they cried:

"Stand up for Kiev, you people of the streets, you smiths

and you farmers and you slaves! Wake up, your time's nigh, take the archers' old places, tear the trestles, stomp the bottles of wine and of mead, and waste all the meat that's been left for the dogs of Batu-khan, the son of Batu. Tear apart the pavilions, take the pikes of the rich, and man the walls of Kiev the great. We won't let Batu-khan, Batu's son have his feast in the streets of the holy city of Kiev. Another feast will he find at the walls. A feast of boiling tar and pitch, of arrows and clubs, of staves and swords and maces.

"Old men, young boys, you women and children! Stand tall at the walls of fair Kiev the great. Some with clubs, some with swords, some with barrels of pitch, and prepare a true feast for the enemies of Rus!"

Then the horde seethed and blustered as it laddered the walls, thinking only of wine and mead and spoils. But the walls held strong, and no wines did they drink, only boiling water, tar, and pitch. Again and again the horde attacked, again and again the walls stood strong, only shaking in the din of that fight.

Then the old men of the city took the front line of defense, and they fought for a night and a day. They pushed back the first wave of the horde of Batu, but they laid down their grey heads in victory.

Batu-khan rages like a rabid dog, and he throws a new wave at the Kievans. Once again the walls shake and buckle, as the waves of the heathen swell like the ocean.

Then the young men of the city took the front line of defense, and they fought for a night and a day. They pushed back the second wave of the horde of Batu, but they laid down their golden curls in victory.

Batu-khan screams in rage like a savage wolf, and he throws his final wave at Kiev. Once again the walls shake and buckle as the waves of the heathen swell like the ocean.

Then, the women and girls took the line of defense, and they fought for a night and a day. They pushed back the third wave of the Tatars to flight, but they laid down their heads in the fray.

Then the walls themselves wept aloud in despair, for no champions remained in the city. The walls, they bent; the walls, they cracked, and a roar rose up in the field of battle. For the gates themselves opened up to the foe, and the enemies cheered as they entered.

But what did they see when they entered the city? All was burnt, all was leveled, no tables of food, no trestles of meat, no pavilions of wealth. For the Rus had destroyed everything that they had. Better nothing remain than it fall to Batu, the son of Batu of the steppes.

And the Tatars, enraged, turned with anger at their chief, and they roared at Batu, Batu's son.

"You called us to Kiev, you called us to Rus, you promised us food, mead and wine! And now we must live like paupers in ashes, for nothing remains of this city of gold."

The Return of Ilya Muromets

꧁ꕥ꧂

D arkness hangs over the lands of the Rus, thicker than
the murk of night. In that darkness, in that blackness
where no light abides, where the paths and the roads are
impassable, look! There, in the darkness of night, a woman
hurries, a young lady walks without fear, without worry. She
rushes to Ilya Muromets in his bondage, an emissary to a pris-
oner. In her right hand—a cloth-a-gold bag, in her left—an urn
of gold. In that bag she bears bread, the mother of foods, in
the urn—the mead of the fields.

Avdotia Riazanochka found the fissure that held Ilya
Muromets. She cried to that darkness with a voice like a bell:
"Hear me, Ilya Muromets, answer me true. How go your days?
How live you your life?"

And she heard from the depths this answer:

"My life is a breeze, a den of repose! It's not bread that I
eat, but the pure air itself, and not mead that I drink, but the
raindrops from heaven. I have a bed softer than feathers of
down: the bones of the earth made smooth by my back. For a
pillow I have my own warrior's arm, and for clothes the dew of
the morning. Every night, I sleep without waking at all, every

day I take Sviatogor's sword, and I strike at the stones, making stairs of these rocks. Soon I will climb to my freedom."

Batu-khan, Batu's son in Kiev sat, thinking wolfish thoughts in his head.

"All of Rus," he said, "lies in bondage to me. Ilya Muromets rots in the earth, dead from hunger and thirst. My armies are greater than any that walked on this earth from the dawn of time. Should I not take my leisure and walk about on this earth which belongs to me?"

He called his slaves and his warriors true: "Hear me, dogs of the steppes, listen to my words. Go and hurry to that tomb for the living, that hole in which Ilya Muromets found his doom. Go and bring me his bones, glimmering white in the moon. His skull I desire, the head of that warrior, to fashion a cup for my wine."

Then they hurried, those slaves of the dog of the steppes, but they hurried right back even faster.

"Hear us now, Batu-khan, Batu-son of the Steppes. For a miracle we've seen, a wonder we've heard. Ilya Muromets himself sings songs of the Rus and promises to scythe us like wheat. And we saw that he hewed the bare bones of the earth with a sword as sharp as can be! He saw us a moment, and promised us, saying, 'Soon I will climb to my freedom!'"

Batu sat still, Batu-khan sat calm as he said, "Rus is dead, without glory. No power remains, it will never arise, and for aeons I'll be its own master. Only this fool Ilya, he alone remains. A thorn in my side for all time."

And he called on his warriors, his strong ones, his sons: "Hail to you, warriors of grasslands and hills! Take your chains and your ropes and your iron bands. Tie the strong man up, bring his carcass to me, and I'll give you a gift fit for kings."

But his sons and his warriors stood agog, for his gifts held no interest, no joy. For to tie up Ilya: that meant death without doubt, but to court the wrath of Batu—even worse! Who would solve this dilemma for them?

Then a wise man among warriors, a cunning magician named Tarakhan Tarakhanovich stepped forward and said, "O lord of the world, the king of all that lies under sun! I humbly kiss the toes on your feet, so listen to the words that drip from my tongue. There is no one among us as strong as Ilya, none to challenge the man from Murom. Though with strength we will fail, all is not lost, for with cunning we'll chop down this willow. Hear my word: set a watch all around that fissure day and night, so that not even a deer or a rabbit can come near, nor a falcon or duck approach from the sky. Then Rus's people won't help nor aid their hero with food or with drink. For soon, the man's power will wane, and then, we will bring him to you, to kiss your heels, to lick the dust off your boots."

No sooner said than done.

And the rumors returned to the ears of Batu:

"First he railed and thundered, this warrior of old, striking with sword and with song. But a week passed, then two, and no more did he rail. A wheeze in his voice, a tremor in his hand, and now we hear nothing at all. Either dead is Ilya, or near it enough. Prepare, great Khan, for your guest!"

Batu-khan, Batu-son rejoiced at the news, and commanded that Ilya be fetched. "Be he living or dead, bring him here to my feet, so my heel can rest on his forehead."

And the horde brought Ilya to the feet of the Khan; they harried and hassled and bound him with ropes. A trussed-up chicken he looked and he felt as Batu chortled over his form.

Batu-khan rejoiced in his blackest of hearts: "You hump-backed old horse, you ass of the hills. What madness to fight against fate! For lord of the earth I am fated to be, and there's nothing that you or Vladimir can do. So, what should I do with you? Impale you or skin you? Or break your back in two?

But no, I will spare you, Ilya of the Rus. Go ahead, my dogs, untie the great man!"

There he stands, barely able to keep upright, fair Ilyusha the son of a farmer.

Batu-khan spoke soft words, "You are old, Ilya Muromets, you are tired, abused, and unloved. Don't you know that I've heard all that Kiev has done to its favorite son and warrior true? They are vermin. Come, sit with me, feast at my table. I will make you my right hand. I will shower you with gold if you serve me and nobody else."

But Ilya only screamed with his warrior-voice, "You dog with no tail, you mongrel Batu! You can't buy bogatyri with gold or with wine. We are Russian, and we serve till the earth takes our bones. While I stand and breathe I will fight you and smite you, till the smell from your horses is lost from our lands."

Then Batu regretted his tender concern, and he threw Ilya out of his sight.

"Take him, bind him, throw him back to the hole that's him home from this day."

And they tied him, they bound him, but Ilya would not stop, and he called back for Batu to hear, "Get away from this land, you dog Batu-son, clear this land of your reeking horde, only then will you live!"

Batu had enough. His rage took his mind from his head clear out. And he spit in the eyes of Ilyusha the brave.

"Oh you Russians, your boasting, your crowing! Even as you expire, my foot on your neck, you still pretend you're a victor? What a braggart you are, you and all of your kind. Well, enough!" He commanded, and turned to his slaves. "Have his head cut off by morning!"

And they took Ilya to the fields of war, where the bodies were sown like wheat. Even further they bore him, to the fields of Kulikovo, to a headsman's block made of aspen. And they forced his head, already so grey, to be bent for the headsman's axe.

But Ilya had enough. His anger boiled over, his heart caught fire, and his limbs filled with strength. He shrugged his shoulders, and the chains cracked in half, clattering to the ground in a heap. He tore all the ropes, and he broke all the bonds, then he looked at his captors and smiled. Taking the block of aspen wood, he stood up as straight as he could. Then he swung, and like flies his captors fell, like stalks of beans in the winter. They lay down and died, and Ilya rose up, and he prayed his thanks to the Lord.

Then he turned to the sun, and in wonder he sang. For the fields of Kulikovo were full. Like a harvest of barley, the bogatyri had come. Dobrynia Nikitich, Nikita the Tanner, Aliosha, the son of the priest. All the warriors of old stood together that day, and they turned with their blades toward Kiev.

And the hordes of Batu were disposed of like rats, and the dog's cursed armies were routed. Batu-khan ran away, his tail between his legs, and Vladimir ruled again in Kiev.

For a season or two, the people of Rus enjoyed fair weather and peace and joy. But the sunset of omen appeared in the sky as the Tatar horde gathered again. But the final fight with those dogs of the steppe would not come for a year and a day.

In the meantime, fair Kiev rebuilt its white walls, and Vladimir feasted from morning to night. The warriors guarded the roads and the ways, and Ilyusha took rest from his labors.

He remembered the words he had heard in his youth from the wandering healers of old. "Go to battle with God," they had said to him. "For no living warrior will deal the blow that sends your soul from its body."

Acknowledgments

A huge, warm thank you to all my patrons who have made the podcast and this book possible.

Without you, I would not be able to do half the things that I do. You empower me to create freely, and that is the greatest gift you could give.

Thank you!

As promised, I thank each of you by name in person:

David Land
Harrison
Michael Schaub
Dion Roddy
Kathleen Knierim
Joyce Lee
Chris Schwegler
EvanG
Nathan Condon
Mark
Logan Meeks
Monica Olsen
Marquelle Anderson
Dakota Baker
Jennifer Adams
Philip Latimer
matthew a whiteford
Melanie Froese
Basil Thompson

Sean Malczewski
Mary P
walrusking14
Gregory Doyle
Erin Turner
Sara Silkwood
Milan Hanacek
Shirley Chui
Donna Loomis
Sherry Shenoda
Craig Malpass (Maniphesto)
Dominic Palermo
Laura E Wolfe
Llana Kyriake Tadros
Moses Rhys Pasimio
Paul Lloyd Robson
Mary Ellen VanMarter
Benjamin Wood
Julie Paine
Julia Houck
Roman Glass
Helen Terry
Vesper Stamper
Danny Van Orden
Eline
Christian
Wendy Haught
Philip Hallstrom
Fabiola Quezada
Jeremy Morgan
Alexander
Aleksey Paranyuk
Adam Lowell Roberts
George Renninger
Sarah Albright

Kathy Butler
Petri
Ryan Harbry
Cole Pero
Steve Nicksic
Bonnie JUDY
Katie Newberger
Beau
Leighton Jack
Jose
Catherine Barrett
Garrett Widner
Jon Eriksson
Steven Luber
Noelle Bartl
Jonny Walker
Annie Turano
Samuel Derkatch
Jack Keoseyan
Eleni Tsagaris
Jacob Russell
Remington Sloan
Theodore Cooke
Konstantin Graf
Алексей Ковинский
Anastasia Brodeur
Brianna Henderson
Jesse Rimshas
Fr. Matthew Smith
Gabriel Wilson
Aham Svarupa
Nina McDonald
Patrick Wilcox
Robin Morris
Julie Gould

Steve Litteral
David Moser
Mary Maceluch
ChristianRPG
Zoe Turton
Daniel Austin Burnett
Joachim Wyslutsky
Svetlana Birthisel
George Luimes
Marlo Orlovich Perry
Kevin Zalac
Stephen Jones
Tim Andrews
Angel
Tim M Dwyer
Dn. Andrew Wilson
Ben Andrus
culianu
Fr. Anthony Perkins
John Considine
Nicholas Medich
Robert Hegwood
Blake Paine
Jo Navarre
John Simmons
Elise Roberts
Zoe Kaylor

Also by Nicholas Kotar

About the Author

Nicholas Kotar is a writer of epic fantasy inspired by Russian fairy tales, a freelance translator from Russian to English, the resident conductor of the men's choir at a Russian monastery in the middle of nowhere, and a semi-professional vocalist. His one great regret in life is that he was not born in the nineteenth century in St. Petersburg, but he is doing everything he can to remedy that error.

Made in the USA
Monee, IL
20 May 2024

58662467R00049